INTERRACIAL SEX COLLECTION

COLLECTION

EXPLICIT DIRTY EROTICA SHORT STORIES

TRISTA JACO

plicit Press

CHAPTER 1

CHRISTMAS GIFT

IT WAS a few days before Christmas and Karlie Mahoney had finally asked her secret crush out on a date. Dinner with Andy Carter had gone exactly as she had planned. Karlie had been attracted to Andy for a while now. She fantasized many nights about having his chocolate brown complexion against her lily-white skin, their bodies sweating from passion. Andy was everything she wanted in a man; tall, dark, handsome, intelligent, and the list went on and on.

He worked as her realtor and when her divorce became final, he helped her move into her new apartment. As they finished dinner, she invited him back to her apartment to chat a little.

As they walked along the joyful streets, everyone seemed to be celebrating and passing on the Christmas cheer. As they waited for the elevator on their way up to her apartment, a warm feeling lingered in the air. The elevator finally arrived. Karlie pressed the button for her floor and before the door had fully closed, they were at each other, hands groping, mouths seeking each other. Andy felt Karlie grab his cock, grunting as she squeezed him hard. He had gotten his hands beneath her blouse, delighted to find she was not wearing a bra and began squeezing her breasts, crushing them with his hands, making her moan against his mouth.

The soft chimes of the elevator interrupted them and they pulled apart. Karlie led him down the hall to her apartment, managing to get the door unlocked as Andy held her, darting his tongue into her ear, practically dry humping her in the hall.

Before the door clicked shut they were at each other again. Karlie dropped her purse on the floor, the keys skittering off under the hall table. Andy shed his top just as quickly as she did hers, both of them kicking off their shoes. They were instantly locked in a deep kiss, lips brushing against each other, tongues thrusting back and forth. Andy again ran his hands beneath her sweater, pulling it up and over her head, her hair crackling with static, as she pulled her skirt down over her hips.

They hadn't even gotten a moment to utter a word to each other. They were too consumed with their passion. For months the chemistry between them had been becoming stronger and stronger. Tonight was finally time to consummate their passion.

. . .

Karlie was maneuvering the zipper and button on Andy's pants, eager to get at his growing erection. She pulled his pants and boxers down, his cock springing out once free of his clothes. He'd gotten rid of his own light sweater, adding it to the pile on the floor. He stood naked before her, his cock large and hard, sticking straight out in front of him.

He looked at Karlie, standing in only her panties, staring down with wide eyes at his cock. He wanted to know what she was thinking, particularly if she had any doubts.

"Do you like what you see?" Andy's voice was low. Karlie nodded, her lips parted, never taking her eyes off his cock.

"Would you like me to fuck you with my cock? To pound you, fill you up with it?" She nodded again. "Touch it, Karlie, reach out and stroke my cock. Feel how big it is." He wasn't sure if he'd actually said those words or sent a thought to her, but he wanted her to touch him; standing there, being watched, without being touched, stroked in some way, was driving him crazy.

Karlie reached for Andy's cock, taking it in her hand, stroking it slowly. Andy groaned, rocking his hips back and forth. He watched her hand working his cock, sending fire up the shaft. His body ached to fuck her; he was still trying to get past the walls he'd put up over the past weeks. He made it a policy to never have any sexual relations with any of his clients. But Karlie was different. She had something special about her. Maybe it was the way she laughed at his jokes or the way she would stare at him, with those gorgeous doll eyes. He had to admit he was smitten by Karlie and couldn't help what he did around her.

Finally, Andy could stand it no longer. He grabbed her hand, pulling her away from his cock. He spun her around, pushing her up against the living room wall. They crashed against a small table; a vase toppled off, shattering on the floor.

Karlie gasped, looking over her shoulder with large eyes, her hands braced on the wall. Andy saw her eyes darken with passion and he focused his attention on her gorgeous slender body. He stripped down her panties, hearing them tear in the process, the delicate fabric coming away in his hands. He tossed them aside.

Grabbing her hips, he pulled her back toward him, making her bend at the waist. He forced her legs apart with his knees, exposing her pussy to him. He ran his hand between her legs, feeling how wet she was.

Holding his cock with one hand, he rubbed the crown against her slit, coating the tip with her juices. Bracing himself, he entered her in one thrust, feeling her gasp beneath him. She momentarily lost her balance; he grabbed her hips, holding her steady.

. . .

As she regained her balance, Andy thrust into her, driving himself to the hilt into her wet pussy, grinding his hips against her ass, feeling her take all of his cock. He pulled back, looking down to watch his slick, glistening cock sliding out of her wetness. He pushed forward again and again, harder each time, forcing her almost to a standing position with her face against the wall. Andy locked his arms around her hips, pulling her away from the wall, his great strength keeping them both upright. He spread his legs and bent his knees, using his hips to drive his cock repeatedly into her pussy. Karlie was powerless to respond, her feet barely hitting the floor. She had no leverage and was at Andy's mercy.

Andy was grunting with each thrust, pumping hard, as his orgasm suddenly burst from his cock. He screamed, head back, thrusting forward again and again as his cock pumped his load into her. He was dimly aware of Karlie coming in his arms and felt her shuddering against his chest. He was panting, covered with sweat, as he set her feet on the carpet.

Karlie stumbled away from Andy, leaning against the back of a nearby chair. "Wow. I've never...no one has...that was amazing." She straightened, standing in front of Andy. "Would you like to spend the night?" Andy was slightly surprised but very pleased, at her offer. He pulled her to him, kissing her forehead. "I'd love to."

. . .

Karlie was asleep within minutes. Andy was wide awake, trying to be patient, waiting until he sensed she was dreaming. Her gorgeous blonde hair flowed onto the pillow and her naked body seemed to thank him for satisfying her to the point of total exhaustion. A soft smile touched Andy's lips. She was his beautiful Christmas present.

CHAPTER 2

COCO AND THE REDNECK

COCO ARCHED her lower back and guided her dark, short fingers over her thin, short clit. She moaned. Luckily the shower water drowned out her passionate self-embrace. Coco didn't want any of her new Sorority sisters to know she missed her ex-boyfriend's steady, thick strong cock meat. She spread her fingers wider. Each of her blood-engorged labia lips slid in between two fingers. She squeezed her hand. She answered the erotic feeling pulsating from her cunt by shaking her pussy lips. Shake four times sideways. Stop. Shake four times sideways. Stop.

Coco's routine usually got her off in three minutes flat. Already she had taken too long. Brandy, the Sorority President, always used the shower next. Coco wanted some thick meat between her short thunder-thighs. She planned to buy a small lipstick size vibrator to sneak into her morning shower routine. She had a bubbly personality. Coco's dark chocolate skin contrasted wildly with the blonde, fair skin sisters in her new sorority. Last year, somehow, Coco made it into the prestigious sorority that ran the Great Kansas University social life. Her white sorority sisters loved her and finally accepted her. She proved she did not harbor anything against white boys by fucking one. That was her final challenge during pledge hell week. Eric, the white boy she fucked, graduated and went off to the peace corp. Now Coco felt alone again.

At their weekly sorority meeting, Brandy announced. "Our prestigious brothers have a legacy that is," she coughed, preparing her sisters for the words. "A redneck."

"A legacy, a redneck." Jane Madison, one of the super-model blondes, and last year's Homecoming Queen said. "I know who you're talking about," she didn't even look up from filing her long manicured nails.

"Do I know him?" said Cindy,

"No Cindy Brady!" All the sorority girls said, mocking the blonde who looks strikingly like the girl on the Brady Bunch 60s show.

"I know him," Cindy said after giggling. "It's that Mohawk guy walking around looking at every girl's ass."

Coco said, "That would be Joel. He's in my art film history class." "Ewwww a freshman taking art history class already," Elizabeth criticized.

"I agree, he must be pretty dumb to already be trying to up his grade point average." Brandy concluded.

Jane Madison pointed with her nail filer, "Coco this is your chance to return a favor." Coco snapped, "No."

Jane Madison, replied, "Yes!"

All the fair-skinned blondes said together. "Yes! Yes! Yes!"

"I don't want to do it. I proved I wasn't prejudiced last year when I fucked Eric." All the girls said, "And you fell in love, too!"

"Mere accident. Eric had class. Joel has no class!"

Cindy and Elizabeth high-fived, and said, "Yep, Joel is a Redneck,"

"Now don't be so proud." Brandy calmed them down. "Each one of us knows what it's like to be alone; away from our comfortable social peers. Joel is pledging our prestigious brother fraternity this month. He deserves the same chance as Coco."

That decided it. Coco's emotions flew every which way. Fucking Joel didn't fall under optional. She did want some cock. *But ewwww!* she thought, going up to her room. *What if he really is a Redneck?* She plopped down on her bed. She held back her tears. She snaked her hand down to her empty fuck space, clutching, convulsing around the emptiness. She rolled on her back and reached for her big vibrator. She hopped up and locked her door, keeping Cindy out. She fucked herself with her cucumber vibrator. She came loud and hard knowing at this hour their fraternity brothers next door always played loud music.

Coco's window lay in a horizontal plane across from Eric's old room. She thought about tall, blonde, big cock Eric and fucked herself more. She penetrated the depths of her cavernous hole. She rocked her hips, locked her ankles and her pussy quaked all over the cucumber toy. Then Coco relaxed.

After ten minutes, she heard a loud annoying voice. "Howwwdddeeeee! Anyone home over there!"

Coco jumped up. She forgot to cover her big chocolate DD cup tits.

"Ohhhh heaven, the cows have gone to university," Coco heard the irritating voice say. "I saw them milk knockers, cutie."

Coco ducked below the windowsill. The voice had bright red hair, a ton of freckles, and none of them formed any acceptable pattern on his skin. They were randomly thrown everywhere on his face.

"I saw you, black beauty."

Coco had enough. "My name is Coco and I am not a horse!"

Joel stayed quiet. He said in a low voice, "In times like these, we need all the friends we can get. I apologize."

"Thank you!" Coco said and slammed her window to avoid his nauseating voice and manners again.

Brandon came over and talked to Brandy. Both lead their fraternity and sorority. The two were engaged to be married, too.

Brandon said, "Time to return our favor."

"Coco already agreed," Brandy said, turning to Coco sitting there in her white towel.

A day later, all the fraternity brothers arrived to the girl's sorority house wearing fake black Mohawk hair wigs.

"Joel can't remove his Mohawk until after the Homecoming Dance tomorrow tonight. We're showing him how stupid a Mohawk really looks in college."

"You mean I have to fuck him wearing that..."

"That's not so hard," Brandon said, "You look really

nice with your straight shag hairstyle. Let us remember, Eric fucked you with your afro, Coco."

Coco crossed her short black legs. "I can do it. One for the team." Her sorority sisters made their trademark secret yell.

"It's all decided," Brandy said, This Friday, before the dance. We'll see if Joel really is a Redneck."

Brandy and her sorority sisters waited for Coco to come down in her white and black checked bath towel. Brandon and his fraternity brothers, along with Joel waited too. Joel waited in a green and yellow towel, his fraternity colors.

A small pink air mattress lay on the living room floor. The six o'clock alarm rang. On cue, Coco came down the stairs. She tried not to look nervous. She stopped on the steps and yelled out the Sorority secret yell. Her sisters backed her up.

Coco said, "I feel much better now."

Joel went forward, and Brandon ripped away from his towel. Joel, caught off guard, covered up his dick.

Coco stopped walking forward. "Are you ready?"

Joel made a deep bow and curtsey. "Yes, my lady. I am ready to bed you. And shall we have many happy heirs to the throne?" He removed his hands from his dick and balls.

All the frat boys yelled. "Go, Joel!"

Coco lay on the pink air mattress. She unfolded her towel. She combed her hair. She waited. Joel went forward. Everyone held their breath.

He held himself up by his right hand and knee as he lay down on top of Coco. He positioned his seven-inch banana dick at the apex of Coco's dark–chocolate pussy. He stared into her eyes. He pushed as Coco willingly opened herself open and raised her legs, locking them on Joel's back.

They started fucking. Each stroke left the Greek girls

and boys feeling warmer and warmer toward one another. Each time Joel withdrew, the strain on his face increased. The strain on Coco's face lessened.

"You're cock's a nice size," Coco finally said.

Joel said, "And you are not ordering me around crushing my balls—like they say black girls do." Finally, they got to fucking in earnest. Everyone got so horny that everyone paired off boy to girl.

They joined Coco and Joel on the black rug. Soon the house filled with mewing from the
women and grunting from the men. Until everyone had a massive climax. It was over.

Brandon said, "Joel you pass the Fraternity's final test."

Brandy said, "Coco, you don't have to date him. You can date whoever you want."

Coco smiled happily with her orgasms. "I'm willing to try another black-white relationship, Joel are you willing to try your first one?"

Joel said, "Wait until after I mow down this silly Mohawk. " Everyone showered, dressed, and went to the Homecoming. Everyone had a good time.

CHAPTER 3

DOIR'S BLACK GIGOLO MAN

DOIR LAY ON HER BACK. Her left leg was up in the air. Her clit jutted out, hard and excited. The redheaded shapely woman lay on her silk sheets on the bed of her lush house. She was naked, unashamed. A small tuft of red pubic hair pointed to her pulsating clit. Her pussy lips were gooey from her moist juices. Large silk pillows propped up Doir's upper back as her blue eyes focused on Tim's helpless brown eyes.

"How much am I paying you an hour?" she asked.

"One thousand dollars," Tim replied, waiting on his knees. His white dress shirt was unbuttoned, his black bow tie hanging around his neck. He looked like a child in a candy shop told to stop, right before he reached in and grabbed some candy. His huge muscles tensed. His six-pack abs were flexing; holding his position on his knees on the soft bed took more upper body strength than he imagined.

He wanted to lay down on Doir. He had fantasies about giving Doir cunnilingus. He didn't start off interested in being a submissive. However, when he heard one thousand dollars an hour, he couldn't resist.

Doir forced him to obey her. She loved stopping all his powerful muscles at a word. She relished her power. She needed to display her power to control Tim. Each moment Tim waited, he gave in. His pride dwindled away. His macho belief meant nothing. If he wanted his money, he dare not do anything Doir didn't ask.

Doir slowly raised her manicured and burgundy painted toes. She let her foot trail up his strong straining thighs. She lightly tapped his pool-ball-sized sacs. Tim flinched like she had Karate kicked his balls. It was not her force, but his heightened sensitivity to her lust and his own frustrated desires that made him flinch.

Doir raised her foot higher letting the front of her toes trace his eight-inch-thick caramel-colored cock. Up higher and higher she raised it until her toes were covered in Tim's precum. His clear precum made her burgundy toe color shine brighter.

"You're my fuck slave." "I am."
     Doir flexed her ankle until the balls of her feet and toes lightly slid across Tim's naked six-pack abs. She moved the balls of her feet across his almost hairless-caramel chest. A few tightly curled black hair circles were unable to stop her foot's upward advance.

. . .

Doir knew Tim could smell the perfume now wafting up from her thighs and the V of her crotch. She raised her foot higher and touched his neck. Tim had no Adam's apple. Doir liked that.

She touched his chin with her foot and slowly pressed down on it.

She opened his mouth with the ball of her big toe.

Tim sniffed. He loved the smell of Doir. He didn't have to say it, but Doir knew eventually he'd be unable to resist.

"I love the smell of your feet and legs. You smell like mangos, flowers, and earth."

"I'm horny, Tim." Doir's pretty peds reached Tim's mouth. "Open wide my black lover."

Tim opened his mouth and Doir slipped her foot inside it. At this point, Tim couldn't hold back. His dick had hardened to an unbelievable stiffness. His balls beat rhythmically under the base of his dick, calling for his sperm to rush out. Tim's tongue slipped out and in between Doir's big toe and second toe. He licked her big toe. He licked her feet.

He did all this without his hands.

Doir relented. "Use your hands. Hold, lick and caress my feet. My lover."

. . .

Tim sighed, as finally he could make love to her pretty white feet. Her perfectly mango smelling soft feet. He treated Doir's feet as if they were her balloon breasts. She flexed her ankle really slow, guiding Tim to lick lower.

Tim licked the sole of Doir's feet. Doir realized all those pedicures and loofa sessions in her bubble baths paid off big time. "You'll never forget me, Tim. Will you?"

Tim's face strained. He grunted as Doir raised her right leg pushing along his spread, straining thighs.

Tim put his entire mouth around Doir's heel.
    Doir's right leg touched his heated balls. She raised her foot higher and trailed the underside of his huge black dick before gripping the head of Tim's cock meat and squeezing hard, soft, hard, soft, hard, and soft.

Until Tim's six-pack abs moved rapidly inside and out, inside and out and his penis erupted into a long ropy string of white goop that Dior caught between her toes. She kept her vice grip on Tim's penis. His fuck rod convulsed again. Another glob of white man goo tried to get past Doir's peds but failed. Finally, Doir let the last spurt of man sauce fly into the air and hit her right on her forehead.

Doir smiled. "Thank you, Tim," she said as she reached up in her feminine, graceful fashion. She wiped the white spunk on her long, delicate finger. She opened wide her pretty lips and enclosed her finger in her mouth and sucked her finger clean.

Tim sighed heavily.

Doir said, "Thank you, Tim. That will be all for this week. Will you return next week for another session?"

"Yes, Mistress Dior, even if you paid me less I would come. I love you now. I am in your grasp forever."

Tim lowered her foot to the floor. He turned to leave.

"Thank you, Tim," Doir said. "Pick up the money from Maria. It's in an envelope on the living room table. Don't spend it all in one place. And I expect you here at the same time and place next Thursday."

"I will obey, my Mistress."

Doir watched his tight masculine buttocks leaving her bedroom. She wanted to fuck Tim. She got out her big black mega dildo. She would just have to wait until he was fully trained in a month.

CHAPTER 4

FIELD OF LOVE: GO DEEP

HAILE WAS AMAZED at the intensity of the feelings that Sam ignited in her. As he kissed every inch of her lush body, she shivered with delight. As she lay sprawled naked in the end zone of the dark football field, Haile totally gave herself up to him, a sweet, sensual offering to a man who looked like a god.

The moonlight illuminated Sam enough that Haile could see his handsome, chiseled facial features as he rose above her. His piercing, dark eyes roamed over her pale skin, a hungry look on his face. Haile raised a hand and touched his cheek. She was rewarded with a smile and his full lips placed against her palm.

"Damn, baby, you look beautiful out here in the moonlight," Sam told her as he looked down at her. Haile's blue eyes looked silver in the dim lighting. He ran a hand through her thick, red hair, spreading it out on the grass. It made such a pretty contrast.

Haile smiled and gave a low laugh. "You're such a charmer," she said to her quarterback lover as he lowered himself to kiss her cheek and then her neck. She gasped when he nipped her and then sucked the tiny pain away.

Sam's hot tongue trailed a path down over her collarbone and her left breast until he reached the taut peak. He closed his mouth around it and alternated between flicking his tongue over her nipple and sucking on it. Haile arched against him as the throbbing between her legs accelerated. Her pussy came in contact with his hard thigh that was placed between her legs. She felt Sam's smooth, dark skin graze against her clit and thought she was going to go crazy with desire.

Sam chuckled against her breast then released her nipple. "Seems like someone is really horny."

"I can't help it. You make me that way and you know it," Haile said and laughed.

"Let's see what I can do about that," Sam said. His teeth flashed in a grin and Haile's heart skipped a little.

Sam kissed his way down her body, savoring each quickly inhaled breath and whimper Haile made. No one had ever affected him the way she did, he thought as he nudged her legs apart and settled between them. He knew from past experience that the soft curls that covered her sex were the same ginger as her hair. He pressed his lips to her mound and Haile lifted her hips a little as the contact was so close to where she really needed it to be.

Haile couldn't hold still as Sam spread her lips and lightly stroked her clit with his tongue. It felt so good and she was so horny for him. She'd wanted him from that first day three months ago when she'd seen him across the college campus. From the top of his shaved head to his feet, Sam was incredibly sexy and Haile had wanted him.

She'd pretended to drop her books as he'd walked by, drawing attention to herself. Haile had discovered that Sam was not only sexy as hell but nice to boot when he'd helped her pick them up. The chemistry between them was instant and it hadn't taken them long to get physical.

"Oh, that feels so good," Haile said as Sam increased the pressure a little.

Haile felt the orgasm building and knew it wouldn't be long. She was so ready and Sam was so skilled and knew what she liked that it would happen quickly. She wasn't wrong.

"Baby, I'm gonna cum. I'm so horny and it feels so good. You have an amazing tongue," she told Sam.

Sam didn't stop, just said, "Hmmm," and continued what he was doing. He loved the taste of Haile's pussy and the way her clit felt against his tongue. He flicked a little faster and Haile let out a loud moan.

"Oh, shit! I'm cumming. Sam! Oh, fuck!"

Sam didn't let up, just kept the tongue action going as Haile climaxed and quivered against his mouth. Haile threw her head from side to side as intense pleasure flowed through her. It lasted for long moments, leaving her breathless and limp. Sam stopped and raised his head to look into her eyes.

She smiled at him and crooked a finger at him. "Get that hot, black dick of yours up here."

His chuckle was low and throaty as he straddled her hips and moved up her body that way. When he was close enough, Haile ran her hands up Sam's strong thighs to where his dick hung between them. She played with Sam's ball sac, loving how soft the skin was there, then took his cock in her hands. Slowly, she worked his shaft. Judging from its hardness, she wasn't the only one who was horny.

Sam closed his eyes and lifted his face to the sky as

Haile took him in her mouth. It was warm and wet and her tongue swirled around the head making him groan with pleasure. She tickled the little hole in the head and Sam gasped.

"Oh yeah, girl. You suck me so good," he said.

Haile sucked harder and moved her head faster, enjoying the fact that she was making Sam even harder. She felt his thighs bunch and flex and reveled in his strength. He ran his hands through her hair as she licked down his shaft.

"You know what I want, baby?" he asked Haile. "What?" she answered after releasing him.

"I want you on your knees, ass in the air, ready to receive me," he said playfully.

Haile giggled. She loved it when Sam referred to their love play in football terms. Sam moved off her and she rolled over and got up on all fours. Sam slapped her ass and she jumped and hollered in surprise then laughed. Sam ran the tip of his dick down her wet slit and her laughter ended in a moan as it hit her clit.

Sam knew the feeling and knew he couldn't take it any longer. He needed to be inside of Haile. Slowly he pushed inside, reveling in the sensation of her hot sheath enveloping his cock. She was slick and tight. Haile moaned as he filled her and pushed back into Sam.

Sam's hips began to move in a sensual rhythm, creating sweet friction within Haile. When she whimpered in need, Sam knew it was time to go faster and he increased the tempo. Soon he was banging hard against her ass, encouraged by her female growls and mewls of pleasure.

Haile loved that she could take him all inside and she came as his balls kept hitting her clit. Blissful sensations pulsed inside her and she couldn't keep quiet. Her cries spurred Sam to move even faster. Swiftly the powerful tension built inside Haile again. As another orgasm overtook her, Sam let himself go and grasped Haile's hips as he came incredibly hard. Ecstasy coursed through him for long moments before fading. Sam withdrew from Haile and rested back on his calves to catch his breath.

Haile lay down on her stomach and then rolled over. Sam thought she looked incredibly beautiful naked on the field and he would have loved to start all over again. However, it would be better to get out of there before they were caught.

"Damn, girl, that was hot," Sam said as he stood up. He offered Haile a hand up and then kissed her. "We better move it."

Haile giggled and said, "Yeah, I don't want anyone coming around while I'm stark naked. But let me tell you, that gives new meaning to the term, 'go deep'."

Sam and Haile dressed and ran to their car before security showed up. From that point forward, every time Sam played or practiced, he remembered what he and Haile had done on the field and always smiled at the memory.

CHAPTER 5

FILLING EMPTY SLOTS

MONIQUE TRIED to translate the Italian email using Google translate. Running her ex-husband's trucking business appeared easy when she stayed at home, cleaned the house, and cooked his meals. "And the fool Joe had to go and get into the hemp business," Monique muttered to herself. "Like we needed the money." She sifted through Joe's office papers, bills, contracts, traffic routes and reports, a new regulation for the long haul trucks, how many hours each driver was allowed to stay on the road and substitute truck drivers. Truck stops and the list of responsibilities went on and on. Today, Monique wore a safari khaki belted dress and black pumps and yellow hoop earrings. Being the CEO of the business didn't improve her reputation much. For the most part, her truckers assumed she was Joe's sexy new black secretary. Sally was enjoying her two-week vacation. Sally was black and her deep voice sounded similar to Monique's. Whenever Monique worked alone in the office, the white men tried to hit on her. They flirted and talked about her big black butt. Since she rarely came into the office, Monique ignored them. Only now, their flirts about eating blackberry pie, and loading deep docks began to make her horny.

Joe used to give random gifts. He snuggled with her. And Joe gave Monique his wood once a week. Saturday makes it eight weeks since she'd fucked! On top of that, most white men didn't want to deal with her "I-wear-the-pants attitude!" She was trying to control her "Pants attitude." But so far, Monique couldn't be certain to get some white dick; even though she ran "Midwest Joe's Trucking." Then, one day, a vibrant, volunteer trucker from Seattle showed up, his guitar strap slung across his broad chest. His checkered shirt tucked tight into his even tighter stonewashed blue jeans. His aftershave, Royal Copenhagen, tipped her over the edge. She had to have this volunteer trucker.

"I heard you have some job openings," Hans said, as he adjusted his guitar and pulled out a folded resume. He handed it to Monique.

She took his resume and unfolded it without taking her eyes off of him. Monique stared at his white-blonde hair. His steel-blue eyes. His wide smile. She looked down at his resume. "Hans. Yes. We have an opening right here in Indiana."

"That's even better." He paused. "I really need this job. I'm willing to do anything wholesome to get the job." He sat down in the ripped gray leather chair in from of Monique's desk. "Sometimes, I need a person to take a truck out to someone stranded or with a flat. Other times, I might need you to stay late and help with the accounting paperwork . . . while Sally is on vacation.

"I am trying to get away from accounting—"

Monique laughed for the first time in weeks. "You're cute. It's not hard accounting. You'll just be filling in empty slots."

"Excel data entry."

"Exactly," she said in a slow, understanding commanding tone.

"Long as it's not too complicated. I just want to drive, and play my guitar at truck stops at night."

"This isn't a worrisome position." Monique extended her palm. "You can handle it." Hans smiled. He shook Monique's hand.

"You can start right now," she handed him the document from the Italian production company. "What does this word mean?"

Hans knew right away. "Spoilage, uhm, product sitting around in the truck." "That is serious."

Hans replied, "A rogue trucker is a canary in the coal mine."

"You may have a new route by Monday." Monique bit her lip as she looked at Hans. She thought I knew Andy was sitting around drugged out on his route. Now we have to pay $2,000 in damage merchandise fees. Monique turned around and checked the wall map of the 50 states. She pointed. "Illinois by now. You ready to go on your first substitution?"

"Yep." Hans stood up. "Just give me a truck."

"I'm going with you," she uttered to Hans' surprise. "I can handle it."

"It's not your problem." She grabbed her expensive

Bayswater Purse. "Let's go." Hans asserted himself, "I'm driving."

Monique smiled and closed the door to the office as she watched Hans' tight small butt.

Hans drove along I-45 West. "If we move at the speed limit, we'll catch him by morning." "I plan on catching him tonight," Monique said, and smiled, "Step on it."

"Whatever you want. There's a long-isolated stretch coming up." "Yes."

When Hans turned onto the Southwestern stretch, Monique unbuttoned her Khaki Safari dress. She said, "It's hot in here."

"I'll roll down the window. It's still Indian Summer."

Monique looked out into the dark stretch of lonely highway. "I often think about my guys being out here all alone. Whether their wives or girlfriends are thinking about them."

"Not a problem for me I'm single."

Monique moved closer to Hans. She put her palm on his right thigh. "Does that door lock properly?"

"The door latches just fine, but my pussy flaps don't lock." "I—Uhm."

"Hans you're not a virgin are you."

"I—I just never did it with a black woman before."

"We have juicy cunts that look like blackberry. Blackberry Pie."

"Sounds delicious." Hans finally took his eye off the

road. "I find you attractive as a new fuck— but I can't sleep with a married woman." He shrugged his shoulders.

"I'm single, Hans."

"You divorced, Joe?"

"Joe will be gone for a long time. In order to keep the business, I had to divorce him."

Hans relaxed. "In that case....." He put his right palm on top of her left palm on his thigh. Monique moved her hand inside his thigh. She moved it closer to his crotch. She moved it on his crotch up near the zipper. She turned her shoulders to face Hans and used both hands to free his burgeoning white cock. "Oh, you must be in great pain." She licked her big black lips. "Not to mention your balls all hot and steamy, boiling. That's not good, Hans."

Monique had Hans' six-and-a-half-inch dick out and his pool-ball size fertility sacs in her hands. The wind blew on his naked groin. He turned to Monique and her cleavage looked three inches deep in her unbuttoned khaki dress. "You've got huge dark nipples."

"Black grape tits." Monique practically hummed. "She lowered her head onto Hans' lap. Her tongue eased onto his bulbous dickhead. She liked the silky feel of his small cock. "Don't worry about your size, Hans. A smaller dick means I have more control." She licked and swirled her tongue around his dick meat. She pushed Hans's pink dick deeper into her mouth. She let her tongue slide under the base of his cock and nudged his dick crown past her gag reflex

. . .

Hans moaned. "I can't drive like this. We have to stop."
Monique ordered, "Pullover by the next traffic sign."

Hans kept closing his eyes and his voice stuttered. "I'm
not going to make it."

"Let it go, Hans," Monique's head bobbed up and down
going fast as she sucked his cock with an intensity of a virgin
who turned eighteen years old.

Hans pulled over, driving as if drunk down a slight
embankment. "I'm cumming! Suck that candy cane."

Monique's hand circled left as her mouth circled right,
licking, her tongue, kissing and snuggling her thick black
lips around his pale cock. Her big brown eyes looked up at
Hans. Her long straightened black hair swayed on her
shoulders.

Monique took both hands and held Hans' cock tight as he
began to buck and thrust his spurting white glops of fertility
down her deep black throat. He moved his hands on her
head and lightly stroked her hair. He threw his head back,
letting the moist breeze hit his face.

Monique licked his cock one last time. She used her tongue
to flick up the white sperm that spilled from her cheeks.
"There. Feel better?"

"Much!"

"This is just the beginning, Hans. Andy's doing just
fine."

"You made up this excuse—" He laughed. "You played

me like a guitar string." "No really. I mentioned your duties —filling empty slots!"

Hans removed his checkered shirt.

Monique felt up his broad shoulders and down his triangular shape to his narrow hips. Hans grew confident, "I'm happy to fill your empty pussy slot."

"Ass too." She laid back and pulled Hans on top of her. "I'm the hunter, Hans." She unbuttoned her safari dress all the way down. She opened the dress. Her dark curly pussy hairs stared Hans in the face. "Time to contribute to my core needs?"

"Yes, Ma'am".

"Two times a week at first," Monique grabbed Hans' average cock. She eased it into her hot steamy fuck box. "You do this and I'll show you how to fuck my ass next."

"No problem."

"I think, we're going to get along just fine, Hans."

CHAPTER 6

SEXING UP ABRIL

ABRIL CHANGED POSITIONS. Her tiered black wet hair draped her white shoulder. Now she laid butt naked on her left side on her queen-sized bed holding one leg bent high in the air. Her lily-white left hand stroked her throbbing clit over and over. Her pussy lips glistened in the bedroom light. Abril had been chasing the Big O for an hour now. The tension from holding her leg in the air as Mambalisa suggested helped. Abril's nerve endings sensed a new growing tension. Erotic sensations that barely reached from inside her clit to her vagina extended up to her womb and then stopped. Shut off. Soft mystical music played to stimulate Abril's Root Chakra, the chakra for sex. Twenty-three-year-old Abril tried everything Mambalisa suggested at least once.

Mambalisa said previously, "A woman usually can't come because she doesn't feel safe. Or psychologically speaking, she can't release her lust energy. Mambalisa made Abril feel good. "If I were a slut or even a streetwalker, Mambalisa,

You'd still love me." Abril crossed her legs in her short-short distressed blue jeans and tight white strappy blouse. "When I leave here, my sexual juices are sure to dry up."

"If you were not married to Collen, what one thing would you do?" Mambalisa said, writing the session notes.

"If I were single . . . I'd go out and fuck a black man!" She tossed her black hair back, as she sat up on the black leather couch in Mambalisa's office. "I'd get drunk, go into Businessman's Bar and fuck some black guy. Any black guy; the first one who prepositioned me. Black men always want hot-sexual white women to wet their huge whistles."

Mambalisa bit her lip. "Abril, you should be a writer. You're making me hot." "Sorry. I just need some relief. The Big Orgasm."

"I'm going to get you there, Abril. I promise."

Abril got up and straightened her blouse over her belly jewelry. "Collen wanted me to remove my belly jewelry. He says it makes me too sexy for my Luxury High Fashion boutique job." "He's such a jerk."

"I know, Mambalisa." "Abril, just divorce him."

"I want to know if I can work out my sexuality first." "Good. Don't let Collen take power over your sexuality."

"I'm going to prove I can have the Big O by the end of this week."

Mambalisa quietly walked Abril to the office door. "Today is Thursday, Abril. And Friday is the end of the week."

Abril batted her large green eyes twice. She raised her

eyes to Mambalisa. Abril smiled. "Then I don't have much time do I."

"Come to the Sex Institute's Get Together Party tomorrow night."

"Collen ruled that off-limits." Abril sauntered out of the office into the hallway. She shrugged her shoulders. "I'll think of something. Maybe I'll attend."

Mambalisa knew that was highly unlikely based on everything Abril said about not wanting to divorce Collen, her rich doctor husband.

On Friday, Abril waited for Collen to come home. She drank several martinis to boost her courage to drag Collen to the Sex Institute's Get Together Party. Guilt nagged at her every time she tried to call him. His line was busy. He could not be paged either. "He's probably in surgery again. Friday nights were bad for unexpected shootings, stabbings, and hospital emergencies," Abril pouted. She poured herself another drink and put on the blue toga in her closet. She hadn't worn the toga since her wild college days. Parties where people claimed she came, squealed, and had a good time.

Abril took a shower. The day was ending. She powdered on her foundation, even though her flawless peachy skin didn't need it. She put on mascara and she smoked her eyes around the eye line. A dab of brown highlights on her eyebrow line pulled out into points that made her very sexy. She gave off a radiant glow. Earlier that morning, she painted her short fingernails pitch black. "I'm going to achieve the Big O."

. . .

Abril blow-dried her black tiered shag, shorter on the front ends, but longer in the back. She rather be mistaken for a Goth girl with attitude before being perceived as a stripper. After slipping her blue toga over her head, she laughed.

She pulled her gold-purse chain up to her shoulder. She went out the door. She caught a cab and told the Indian driver, "The Sex Institute over on 48th street. By the Businessmen's Bar.

"Sure, you want that?" The Indian driver said, pulling away from the exclusive high-rise apartments. "You seem a little drunk, lady."

"I'm—I'm not drunk." Abril snarled. Her dark-tiered shag hair bounced off her shoulders.

Abril stumbled out of the cab. To the left was the white Sex Institute Building and to the right stood the black Businessman's Bar, a bar whose clientele served middle-class blacks primarily.

Abril decided to let the warm breeze decide her fate. As she neared the sidewalk both buildings sat waiting on, her arms and shoulder tilted toward the bar. "Why buck fate?" Abril said. She took a deep breath. Her legs felt damp between her legs. Just moving toward Businessman's Bar caused her sex cleft to heat up. She felt like a hotplate left on the stove. The hunger games the warm breeze played on her exposed cunt lips fascinated her. She flirted with the first guy leaving to go home. "Is this a good place?"

"Of course," said the African American in his business suit leaving.

When she walked in wearing her toga, all the black guys turned their heads. It was almost as if they smelled the musky sweet scent between her legs mingling with her Pure Romance Basic Instinct perfume. At the bar, Abril ordered a Chardonnay. "Please, bring it to the table." Abril pointed to the empty curved table booth tucked discreetly at the end of the bar.

Sitting nearly naked in a k bar captured her clit's imagination. She waited on a secret dalliance to open. Her senses shifted and Abril turned to see a handsome black man sliding into the booth with her.

"I'm Khaled."

Abril extended her hand.

Khaled moved her soft hand to his lips and kissed it.

"Wow!"

"Mambalisa told me about you."

"Mambalisa?" Abril's green eyes sobered up. "Why?"

"I'm a black man who fantasized about sleeping with a white girl." "You see Mambalisa?"

"I do."

"Why not just go and get one?"

"I work for the City Treasury Department." He said softly, "I'm afraid someone might target me for some scandal."

Abril put her hand under the table and touched

Khaled's slim thigh. "I know no one." "That's what Mambalisa said."

Khaled wore a thinned lined mustache. His hair was close-cut, very conservative. He wore a light blue tie that matched her toga. "Mambalisa said, 'Find the white woman wearing this color.'" He held up the tongue of his tie.

"That's my light blue color."

"And I don't see any other white women in here." "That'd be me!"

"I want you, Abril," Khaled said, letting his hand lightly touch hers. "I won't turn you down, Khaled."

Khaled leaned in and kissed Abril's lips softly. He pulled back and stared into her soft green eyes. "I'm single by the way."

"Perfect! So am I."

"I want to make you cum." "I want the Big O—tonight!"

"Let's go back to my place?"

"Khaled, do it right here." Abril hesitated. "I don't know how much time I have." "Right here!"

"Mambalisa told you I was desperate."

"I don't know--." Wait. He slid closer to Abril. He embraced her again, kissing her deeper. Khaled let his tongue slide over her teeth at first. He started sliding his left hand up along her sexy white thighs. His finger encountered the moisture up near her apex. "You're wet!" "This feels so good, Khaled," Abril said without opening her green eyes.

Khaled said, "Lie back and trust me. You can fall asleep in my arms." Abril's eyes shot open. "I want to cum!"

"You will. I promise," Khaled said as his fingers toyed

and circled the entrance to her sopping cunt. "I want you so bad, Abril."

Abril opened her legs more. Her breathing increased She pushed her small breasts against Khaled's chest. He really seemed more desperate for a white girl, than she seemed for her Big O.

He penetrated Abril and his other hand kept brushing against Abril's neck and dipping to her breasts under the blue toga. Her breasts, braless, were dangling, waiting for the right man's hands to claim their forbidden fruit. Abril grasped when he pinched her nipples. He pulled back and wore a wicked grin of satisfaction on his face.

Khaled's fingers roamed everywhere. He stopped kissing her for a moment and licked her ear. He quietly smelled her perfume. "I love the way you smell, Abril. I'm not going to let you go. I want this to last for months."

Abril sighed. She wanted this confession of passion to come from Collen. Instead, a complete stranger wanted her, needed her body, her presence. She threw her five feet, five-inch one-hundred and twenty-pound frame against Khaled. He almost fell back. His hands raised higher until he had two fingers up her begging, dripping pussy slot and his thumb expertly drumming on her clit. Abril gasped again. "Wait! Wait! I can't just cum all over my dress!"

Khaled lowered his head, freed her right breast from the toga, and sucked her stiff distended nipple into his mouth. He stopped. "You can wear my jacket around your waist afterward." Abril smiled. Her hips started strong thrusting motions. "It's too late now Khaled, I'm coming. I'm coming! Don't stop—"

Khaled gobbled up her passionate release in another big kiss. His tongue searched inside her throat as Abril breathed hard and came, soaking his big left hand. Khaled kissed her until he was sure she would not scream out. Then he stopped. "Thank you, Khaled."

"When can I see you again?"

"I don't know. When I get a divorce." "You would get a divorce?"

Abril pulled his hand from her crotch.

Khaled raised his hand. His brown eyes stared into her green eyes as he sucked her sticky juicy cum off his fingers.

Abril smirked her lips, "You're a very dirty man."

Khaled laughed. "Sex is a messy business, but some-body has to do it."

"That is just the response I needed to hear." She kissed Khaled's pussy fragrant hand. "I'll divorce anyone for you"

"Let's get out of here and go to the Sex Institute, Abril." "Lend me your jacket?"

"My pleasure."

ABOUT THE AUTHOR

Trista Jaco is an emerging erotica author of many erotica kinks and sub-genres. Be sure to check out other books and leave a review if this story got you hot!

Visit my blog at Trista Jaco Blog

Join my newsletter for exclusive Trista Jaco Newsletter

Sign up for Free Stories from Xplicit Press Authors

Xplicit Press Author Updates

Like Xplicit Press on Facebook

Follow Xplicit Press on Twitter

Readers: I want to expand a few of the stories to see where the characters can be explored further. If there are any of the stories that you would like to read more about again, I'd love to hear from you!

Keep In Touch
Trista Jaco
info@tristajaco.com